The GREAT RAINBOW RACE

Adaptation from the animated series: Anne Paradis
Illustrations: Guru Animation Studio Ltd.

Today the Rainbow Kingdom
is hosting its very first Rainbow Race.

True and Bartleby look
forward to participating.
They've even built
their own race car.

All the racers are at the starting line when Grizelda makes a grand entrance in her Griz-mobile, a gigantic race car.

The Rainbow King presides over the race.
"Welcome to the Great Rainbow Race!
The first car to reach the finish line wins!"

RAINBOW RACERS,
START YOUR
ENGINES!

When the Rainbow King gives the signal, all the cars zoom off with True in the lead. But Grizelda passes her and speeds off into the distance.

True, Bartleby, and all the other racers stay close as they chase after Grizelda.

"Racing, racing,
everybody's chasing,"
they all sing happily.

When they come to a turn, no one sees a big pothole on the track. They all hit the pothole and are thrown into a canyon.

BANG!

Inside the canyon, a big boulder falls from the top of the cliff and blocks the way out.

"There's no way out! I guess the race is over," the bus says sadly.

"What are we going to do, True?" Bartleby asks.

"We'll figure it out! But we'll need help from the Wishes," True says.

True calls Cumulo to take her and Bartleby to the Wishing Tree.

Zee listens as True explains the problem. "Let's sit and have a think about this."

The three friends sit down on the mushrooms. They each take a deep breath.

"I've got to move the boulder so that everyone can get back in the race," says True.

"The Wishing Tree has heard you, True," answers Zee. "It's time to get your three Wishes."

WISHING TREE,
WISHING TREE,
PLEASE SHARE YOUR WONDERFUL
WISHES WITH ME.

The Wishes wake up and spin around True.
Three Wishes stay with her, and the others return
to the Wishing Tree.

"What interesting Wishes these are," Zee says.
"Let's see what the Wishopedia tells us about their powers."

SYZER
can make objects
bigger or smaller.

ROPERROO
makes lassos.

CU-BIGGLY
is made of jelly
and is very elastic.

"Thank you, Zee. And thank you,
Wishing Tree, for sharing your
Wishes with me," True says, as
she leaves with the Wishes in
her pack.

When they get to the canyon, True activates Syzer.

ZIP ZAP ZOO!

"I choose you. Wake up, Syzer!
Wish Come True! Make the
boulder smaller."

With the laser, Syzer quickly
shrinks the boulder to the size
of a pebble.
"Thanks, Syzer!" says True.

Now the way to the track is clear for the drivers.
"The race is on again!" says the bus, and she rushes
back onto the track.

The racers are getting close to Grizelda. She decides to activate the Grizmo-turbo to make her car go even faster and increase her lead. This also creates a cloud of dust that lifts the bus high in the air. The bus is stuck in a cactus!
"Help me, True!" cries the bus.

True activates her second Wish.

ZIP ZAP ZOO!

"I choose you. Wake up, Roperroo! Wish Come True! Get the bus down from the cactus."

Using the magic lasso, Roperroo pulls the bus back onto the track.

Meanwhile, Grizelda races along at top speed. But she is going too fast. Suddenly, one of the wheels of her car flies off. Oh, no! She drives off a cliff.

Luckily True and her friends arrive just in time.
True quickly activates Cu-Biggly. The Wish cushions Grizelda's fall. Hooray! She's safe!

The racers concentrate on making up ground. But it's the Forest Flower Kids who reach the finish line first. Grizelda is disappointed. True cheers her up.

"Did you at least have fun?" True asks Grizelda.
"Yes, I guess I did. So winning isn't everything. Who knew," Grizelda admits.

"Congratulations, everyone!" says the Rainbow King. Everybody gathers for treats to celebrate the racers who competed in the Rainbow Kingdom's first-ever car race.

"It's not about who wins, it's about having fun," True says and all her friends agree.

CrackBoom! Books is an imprint of Chouette Publishing (1987) Inc.

Text: adaptation by Anne Paradis of the animated series TRUE AND THE RAINBOW KINGDOM™/MC,
produced by Guru Studio.
Original script written by Tom K. Mason
Original episode #104: Zip Zap Zooooom!
All rights reserved.

Illustrations: © GURU STUDIO. All Rights Reserved.

Chouette Publishing would like to thank the Government of Canada and SODEC
for their financial support.

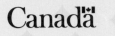

Books
Tax Credit

Gestion
SODEC

Bibliothèque et Archives nationales du Québec and Library and Archives
Canada cataloguing in publication

Paradis, Anne 1972-,

[Course royale. English]
The great rainbow race/adaptation, Anne Paradis; illustrations,
Guru Animation Studio Ltd.

(True and the rainbow kingdom)
Translation of: Une course royale.
Target audience: For children aged 3 and up.

ISBN 978-2-89802-033-9 (softcover)

I. Guru Animation Studio Ltd, illustrator. II. Title. III. Title: Course royale. English.

PS8631.A713C6913 2019   jC843'.6   C2018-942632-2
PS9631.A713C6913 2019

Printed in Canada
10 9 8 7 6 5 4 3 2 1   CHO2052 DEC2018

MIX
Paper from
responsible sources
FSC® C103304